ORACLES:
A PILGRIMAGE

BOOKS BY CATHERYNNE M. VALENTE

THE LABYRINTH

YUME NO HON: THE BOOK OF DREAMS

ORACLES:
A PILGRIMAGE

CATHERYNNE M. VALENTE

PRIME BOOKS

PUBLICATION HISTORY: "The Oracle Alone" & "Los Angeles,"
"Boston," Anchorage," "New Orleans," "Savannah" appeared in
Music of a Proto-Suicide, JAM Pie Press, January 2004; and "Kiluea,"
The Pomona Valley Review, Summer 2003; all others original to this
collection.

Prime Books
www.prime-books.com

for Rene and Sonya

PROLOGUE:
THE ORACLE ALONE

Perhaps you enter a room, cool and dark, tattooed with shadows cast by brocade curtains and sheer veils over the mirrors, the floor stone and cobbled, and perhaps she is there—installed in a demure corner with her feet bare.

Perhaps you think to yourself nam Sibyllam quidem cumis ego ipse oculis meis vidi...it is possible that the tumbling rainclouds and crushed rubies of those ancient words shoot through your mind like a hunting hawk, all sleek wings and talons. You look at her, brushing a long strand of dark hair from her face, and for a moment her profile is the classical phantasm you expected to find. But she is younger than you thought, there are no lines that assure the presence of wisdom, no origami folds in her crane-neck, no silver arrows piercing her hair. She is smooth and curved as the spine of a harp. And now that you have come all this way, the fact of her youth and those liquid eyes frighten you, and you do not want to know what she portends.

She spreads her hands on the velvet table-cover, the light slants in from a dusty window in this high tower, and she is illuminated like a manuscript, a tongue of gold dust and cobalt. You do not want her to open her mouth, you are certain that moths and infant crows flutter within, behind her terrible lips. It is the mouth you fear, that likeness of a door, a crevice sinking deep within blue glaciers. Oh, little one, she wakes all your secret night tremors, she is the serpent chasing you down hallways, she is the drowning sea, she is the mocking moon. Her hands have drawn seven thousand ash-wood bows, and all found their mark in the flesh of your liver. She ululates, undulates, abrades your corneas, from her little corner she bends all the roads you've ever known towards her. If she were old it would be better, you could accept a crone. She would have been less annihilating if you been able to guess the date of her death from the lines on her throat. But it is perfect, long and lithe, and out of it will issue bats singing arias and owls like treble clefs. She is all darkness, enveloped in a body of light so full and thick you could plunge your hands into it and be purified for a century.

She has not moved, but you have, you have orbited her and fallen and escaped and fallen again. She is the fulcrum, and you swing from her like a fat copper pendulum, the arc of you a glowering black line on the floor of the world. Roots have ripped out of your feet and anchored you before her, great thick ropes of her silence diving through the earth like playing seals, and you want to move towards her, but cannot. You have paid your admission and she is yours for the moment, her mouth, round and clear as a crystal ball, is bought, to exhale stars into your palm and tattered asphodels into your chest. It is full of dragonflies. The buzz makes you drunk, and you waver a little, wanting, for a moment, to run and hide in any cavern that will bear you. But that maddening strand, that lock of blackness, the slick of her hair wafting onto her cheek like a bruise, will hold you to her forever. She brushes it away again, uselessly, into the long mass gathered at her neck.

8

You commit the only act which was ever possible, you walk to her, three steps (it had seemed so much farther) and you sit beside her pale skin and dusty green eyes, the shade of a bottle of wine in the cellar. And you do not know why the words which fly up to your tongue like mezzo-soprano sparrows are Greek, except that once in a classroom with a view of the sea you read Eliot and wept. Those same tears fall now, hot and bright as Mars in the summer sky, the secret crimson of passion.

"Σιβυλλα, τι θελεις;"

"Sibyl, what do you want?"

And she inclines her head like a heron, looking at you with eyes full of pity and warning, of oracles and tombs, of oceanic tremors and lunar siroccos. She blurs like an impressionistic landscape through your tears as that seraphim-mouth opens and her voice, voice of blood-maps and continental drift, a voice like the opening of a door. She answers you in that same tongue, vowels like milky breasts and consonants pregnant with swords.

"τεκνον, τι κλαιεις;"

"My child, why do you weep?"

And it begins, and you listen, and she speaks.

THE ORACLE AT DETROIT

The last Michigan Oracle died in 1983. Not knowing
who she might belong to, the citizens
of snow-packed Hamtramck
lowered the corpse down into the bowels
of the Gear and Axle factory, committing
her body
to the deeps.

There, she settled onto a many-toothed gear,
her back arched like St. Teresa transfigured. Her hair
tangled in the ironworks, wrapping itself around
dusty, unused molds empty of plastic, coolant tanks
dripping unnoticed to the spider-laced floor.

Her flesh became green, blotched as though
beaten with ten fists, and then violet,
black veins like ink bursting within her.
Wet skin erupted, sloughed away, and still
her hair grew.

The forgotten levels of the Gear and Axle factory
began to turn towards her
like a field of daisies towards

a bloated sun. The cords of her hair dangled,
slowly bringing mechanical arms around
to hover tenderly over her bones
as though she were a half-built Chevrolet.

And above, in the clang and cough
of the work-floor, a welding arm attacked
the door of a smart red coupe, and wrote
in molten letters, orange and sear:

When all else shall be taken,
A bulwark of wood at the last the heavens allow
sole to remain unwasted,
which thee and thy children shall profit.

And still her hair grew.

From the cap of her skull it descended,
pulling electric cables into her joints,
her eye-sockets, her chest cavity. A second
skeleton spooled out inside her,
sparking and crackling
its black bones. Between the rows
of her teeth, in the cavern of her nose,
filaments nest like flaming cilia,
waving in some unseen wind.

And above, in the clang and cough
of the work-floor, a stitching arm sewed
verses into a driver's seat, white thread on
maroon cloth:

The cast is made, the net spread,
The tunny-fish shall flash in the moonlit night.

And still her hair grew. The web of it
stretched beneath the Gear and Axle factory,
lightless and thick. In the smooth, meatless
cave of her brainpan,
circuits like eyes flashed complexities
at the bone-wall,
and the rust-wedded gears,
dead thirty years and more,
began again their old grind.

The silver robotic arms spread out
like hoplites on the factory floor,
and the line manager saw them arrange
themselves, banging out oracles into
sheet metal, plate glass, hubcaps,
engraved filigree into dashboards
and steering wheels,
stamped into wheelwells,
blazed into still-soft steel.

The prophet-building howled
in its birth, soundless, severe:

I know the number of the grains of sand
and the extent of the sea!
I understand the mute and hear the voiceless!
(O, when the Medes have a mule that is king,
a mule that is king,
a mule that is king,
when the Medes have a mule that is king
The Lydian's feet shall fly!)
The smell has come to my senses
of a strong-shelled tortoise
boiling in a cauldron together with lamb's flesh!
(Ask me not for Arcadia! Ask me not for
acorn-meal! But Tegea, O, Tegea,
Tegea I will give you, wrapped in red rope
like a birthday present!)

And still, her hair grew.

THE ORACLE AT BOSTON

She reads a red leather *Principia Mathematica*
under a smoke-branched blue spruce.
A translucent yellow moth
rests on her feline hair,
the same flutter-pattern as her cavernous eyes.
He glosses the braids with his silent legs—
she drinks from a mason jar of clear water
every third page, and the glass takes an impression
of her lips.

She knows I am supposed to fall in love with her.

I am supposed to take her to see the sculptures of
hermaphrodites at the Museum of Fine Arts,
to touch the small of her back as I remark
that the beatific eyes, the lyric wave
of the hair is similar to hers. And later
there should be gin and tonics overlooking the river
with the lights of cargo ships reflecting in her fingernails.

It is a simple equation, she is supposed to tell me:

$$F = \frac{GmM}{r^2}$$

the force of two objects' gravitational attraction
depends only on their masses
and the distance between them.
When a celestial body approaches another
disturbances are seen in their orbits
like fish leaping in a fountain
thrashing their tales at dark-eyed nebulae.
All she does is taste the ripples as they come
and whisper the length of their arcs.

Her breath would smell slightly of sandalwood and cherry
liqueur.

A gentlemanly brown grasshopper contemplates her ankle—
she removes one silver earring and places it on
Newton's Third Law. I am supposed
to notice the way her fingers massage her lobe—
how they are pale as temple candles.
In fifteen years,
she should be holding me as my throat cracks
like a clay bodhisattva, sobbing
over my mother's grave. In five
she is supposed to break her toe sprinting
up to our fifth floor apartment—the one
with the dove-wing curtains.

She knows—it is all in the book that leaves
red lines on her thighs. She blinks

once, twice,
and the train is 75 seconds early. I have to run
to catch it as the blue and gray doors
slide noiselessly open.

Gravitational disturbances grimace with a flash
of silver tail, and the flick of her frown
erases me as she
replaces her earring
with a practiced hand.

THE ORACLE AT MANHATTAN

eyebrow-ringed sibyl standing blue
in a diner 3 a.m.
she reads your halitosis and your coffee grounds
she reads your cigarette-puffs and your knuckle-cracking
she reads your roast-beef-on-rye-hold-the-mayo
silver rings like wedding announcements
on every finger

purple lipstick twenty four
track marks like a map of Thebes
wears a graduate-school punk half-tee
but in secret she plays jazz trombone
mile high mascara AB neg
she walks shuffling black four-inchers
guillotine-heels wobble but they don't fall down
she reads your soup crackers and scotch
she reads your quiche lorraine
she reads your cobb salad and your nicotine hands
her belly ring all a-glitter
cheap omphalos plastic and red
flashes like a stop light and you leave your pancakes
un-buttered
un-syruped untouched

when she shows you
her pink quaalude-tongue

crayon-black hair
hanging like a murdered cat
syringe-earringed
heroine-angel
streaming liquid mescaline from her eyes
sugar-cube fingernails
tinfoil wings bubbling
she reads your early edition
she reads your tax report
she reads your museums-on-second-sundays palm
leaving ketchup on your fate line
like a sin.

THE ORACLE AT NEW HAVEN

It seemed sanctuary enough.

No one goes up to the second mezzanine, you see—
the pre-Socratics and coarse-cloaked Stoics
stand watch: bi-lingual editions lined up
red and green, like Christmas candles. Only
occasionally would a furtive student
brave those ranks of suicides and emperors,
their fingers twitching across the rows
like an Italian *madre*
caressing a papal tomb.

I think I might have been one of them (I seem
to remember the taste of graphite, the smell
of the card catalogue drifting out of
walnut cabinets—I deduce
that once, I too
avoided these monolithic stacks,
erased my fingerprints
on an industrial typewriter,
memorized the Kings of Spain
from Roderic to Ferdinand) but
I cannot be certain of it. I know

only that I am looking for myself
among the spines of twelfth night;
I was promised
that Ionia recorded the genealogy
of my grandmothers,
that some hexameter existed,
some corrupted Doric noun,
which could tell me
my own name.

I purify my feet every night
in the steel and ceramic Castalia
of the two-stall women's restroom—
the cool blue light
a confessional radiance, closing
my brow in holiness. I am so blank,
so blank,
anything could be written into me;
I would not notice the script.

The graduate students will trade
a tunafish sandwich or a ziploc-ful
of cut carrots for a soothsayer,
smuggle them past the desk clerk
so that I will conjure up
the most advantageous arrangement
of their dissertation committee,
spectacled elders lined up like major arcana—

The Hierophant, Judgment,
The High Priestess.

It is easy work. It leaves me
to long afternoons stitched through
with muted light, huddled
on my black plastic footstool,
squinting at the mantis-calligraphy
of the Adamic Oracle,
her works and days, her
slaughtered snake. Somewhere,

between the geometric angles
of sigma and
the baroque sine-wave of xi,
her name must float—
it must float—
it *must* float—
it must have been written
in the beady organs of the flayed python,
it must have been uttered
by the temple-goats bleating
among granite crags. Surely,
in those first hours,
when the stink of snake-flesh
hung in the air like a ruined flag,
the guilty sun cannot have forgotten
to record her name on his golden belt.

She is there. She is waiting
for my hands to brush
her glyphs, tender
as a daughter.

She is patient.

THE ORACLE AT SAVANNAH

The Eastern sea
like an endless field of crushed lilacs
over stardust. The shore, swept gold
as the knees of her sister
at Delphi,
far-stretched below the balcony,
and the white-silk lilies
with crystal stalks and Old Viennese petals;

(Remember this, and pretend you love me. That
we are not here for her alone.)

Apple, peach blossoms in the scented waters
floating like stockade ships
in honeyed wine. And a single rose like a wound,
flesh as soft as tears.
Is this the grail you sought
on my kitchen table
on the oak nightstand
on the interstate like a black river?

Do you remember how our skin tasted of salt-air and
cane sugar?

(Pretend you loved me once, and lived in the taste of my collarbone. That
you will not ask her whether or not
to leave me.)

My hair, a six-stranded thread
escapes from the dark knot at my neck,
blows like a tin wind-chime against my shoulder.
It is a too-human moment
she cannot touch
that engraves my skin with hissing ink.

Why are we here?
(Why do you shut your eyes? Why will you not open your
hands?)
The ocean is someplace
beyond you and I in this room,
where her voice will crack your ribs
and hold your throat in a white fist.

In this brief scene of deathless flowers
and a sea of gold lipped turquoise
she stands like a caryatid,
stiff-limbed and unyielding
archaic
vicious as a sea of bronze swords.

I do not want to see the petals
of her attendant water
I know what they portend.

Determined, you walk away from me,
towards her,
over the spun straw of the dunes
the sun crowning your hair like a nova.

(Remember. Remember this,
when you stand before her
and her eyes are like abalone shells. Remember
and pretend you loved me once.)

THE ORACLE AT MIAMI

The heat of it blossoms like a night-orchid:
faux-rubies and a shiver of feathers,
the smell of sweat-drenched nylon.
Swinging veils—seven is the traditional number—
yellow as wafts of sulfur,
spangles shaking thyrsus-frantic.
But there is nothing quite so like a cave
as a nightclub, hung with sibyls
dancing undulate in their golden cages,
hair soaked with green glitter, thighs oiled up
like Olympians.

They said it would be all right
so long as I kept to the Blue Room,
and didn't tell anyone. Appearances,
they said, are so important.
What would the others think,
if they knew? Of course,
it is a very convincing costume,
but men are barefoot priests
under the orange-leaved oaks—
they are not Oracles, no matter

how smooth their skin
or cinched their waist.

It is useless to argue
that the bright-haired boy came to me
just as he came to them,
offered a mouth full of laurels and
a lexicon of hexameters,
all the while fingering the jut of my hip
with a glowing hand. He traps us all
this way, makes us his whores,
makes us ridiculous.

No one here comes close
to guessing. My breasts are false
as the Venus di Milo—but I went for the
maidenly model. My lips
are redder than red, my skin hairless,
the line of my jaw gentle enough
to earn me a living long before
the sun came strutting through my door.

They really needn't have worried.
I'd never cast an augur out of uniform.
How do they think I drew
the gaudy-gold eye of heaven?
He prefers the androgyne,
the creature halfway to the moon,

never quite a slave to it.
I wear my scarlet veil, my silver hoop earrings,
strap my feet into yellow snakeskin—
ritual vestments, holy as communion.

        But sometimes,
sometimes, in the dark,
the sweat-dark, full of Chanel and vodka,
a woman in black will come up to my balcony,
and drop her hand into mine. She'll be ashamed
to come to me, the Oracle of the sequin-ghetto,
but I can see the mark
of his scalding fingers on her neck.
        And for her, just for her,
I let my voice drop low and kind.

There is no need for deceit among sisters.

THE ORACLE AT NEW ORLEANS

But for a crab-tooth necklace
she is naked
on a 18th century lemon-brocade chaise
eating peanut butter
from a wooden spoon—
claw marks
of a stray Siamese
bisect her snuff box nipple.
The smell of crawfish etouffee
climbs the iron balcony
like a fevered mouth.

You haggle over price
(she'll only take Haitian gourdes)
while she paints her toenails
the color of unripened tomatoes,
one sugar-cane heel
propped up on your knee.

Her breath hot on your cheeks
a bellow of sour mash and closed tombs,
heavy breasts and sweat-strung hair
brush you like street cleaners,

and the heat, the heat
of her hands clutching you
as if she's the thing boiling
in the silver pot downstairs.

She hooks a finger into your belt
buckle and rasps through her page-turned tongue:

"I am every obscenity
you utter.
You want to smell my hair
cooking
You want to tongue
all my black-bottled moons.
You want my open mouth
thrown in with pickled eggs
floating in a mason jar.

Then you'll run home
to orange juice
and poached eggs
at 8 a.m. sharp,
and forget—

everything but the mouth."

In heat-languor she sprawls,
kneading her buckwheat skin,

legs open as restaurant doors.
She cackles in some throaty
Caribbean tongue—
daring you to take the portents from her
before she has a chance to give them.

But when five crumpled bills
lie like a caesarean scar
on her withered belly,
she unbolts her cracked
tabernacle-mouth
with bored obedience—
places three black rooster feathers
and a drop of palm sap
on her tongue.

They seem to dissolve
into her private convulsion
—cigar smoke in a furnace—
and her eyelids sag
irises rolled back
like grocer's awnings.

THE ORACLE AT AMARILLO

Haruspicy is a family business.

My mother, her mother—
the odd aunt or cousin.
              Occasionally,
a sister-in-law or stepmother will take to it,
caught for a moment in the glisten
of cow intestines on the old oak
butcher's bench.
              Instinctively,
she'll know to pull out the liver,
fat as a brown-bellied river-eel,
and press her fingertip
into the pink blemish
staining the *regiones dirae*
like a mud-trapped starfish.
              But usually,
it passes mother to daughter
to daughter
to daughter
our instructional liver—bronze colossus!—
taken down from the mantle

like a football trophy, and given over from
hand to hand, shriveled to plump.

                Like any business,
records must be kept. I did the books
for my mother for ten years
before she passed the liver. Neat monochrome
columns—slim as Ionians.
36 white heifers this year,
22 black bulls in the pens for next.
Gall-reading for Mrs. Harrison,
lung-scry for Bill Richards,
down on Rt. 66.
                Like any child,
I hated the work. I was sure,
when the time came,
my sister would wear the dress,
lace stiffened and yellow from
so many wearings, pinned and fitted
to all our waists, all our shoulders.

It had to be let out
a full three inches in the bust
for me.

                I wanted
to go to a trade school—
learn computers, maybe,

or automotive repair. Anything
but how to garland a bull's horns
with hyacinth and rosemary,
how to cut left to right
quick enough that they don't scream,
how to scrub out the trough
that catches all that blood,
what to use to dissolve the streaks
of cow-fat clinging to the porcelain.
                    I wanted
to know clean circuits and the process
of making fiberglass—
not the terror-shit
of 36 white heifers per year.
Not the interstices of a severed udder,
not the way their lips curl back from
their wide, flat teeth.

But the liver
came to me, after all.
I wear that awful dress—though
it barely covers my knees.
It's my breath that shows in the morning,
when the snow crusts thin
over the featureless earth. You have to do it
in the morning, you know.
                    The blood
clots faster in the cold.

THE ORACLE AT TAOS

It's all for the tourists, of course.

They come to see an Indian woman
doing a white woman's job. After all,
weren't all the great ones white?
Delphi, Dodona, Cumae:
pasty skin beating a slab of cave
under the sun-god's winged pelvis.

I've got my little crack in the red dirt—
the crack is important, the sulfur
and the laurel (though I've been known
to substitute sage,
and even aloe, in a pinch)—
buried under an afghan
in the back-room of my sister's fetish-shop
stuffed full of obsidian bears and copper Kokopellis
agate turtles and genuine New Mexico turquoise
wolves in mid-howl.
Wheel of Fortune is an orange blare of electric numbers
from my half-brother's television—
he snarls at the eager, O-mouthed customers:

Kokopelli is bullshit. We're fucking Cree.
Why do we have to sell this trash?
Heap big wampum, motherfuckers.

It is what they want, and it is easy.
Just like the novelty
of brown hands on a Rider-Waite deck,
the sheer postmodernity of it all,
the archetypal double-braids, grey as bathwater,
the voice out of a cowboy movie. Once,
a teenager out of Houston asked me to read a scene
from *Fort Apache* with him, just for laughs.

If they can wear a silver Kokopelli around their necks,
with a little diamond in his flute,
then I can sidle up to Apollo,
bat my smoky eyes, sultry as Cumae,
and offer up a gilded throat.
I don't mind shriveling up like a grasshopper,
I tell him, I'm plenty wrinkled and rustled as it is.
I won't go complaining to every damn
6th grade field trip that wanders through.
A cave is big enough—room for my brother's TV
and a few souvenirs:
turquoise omphaloi, a copper Athena or three.

But it's no fun for the mouse-king
if he can't see us cry. I get my cave, all hung

with dusty Navajo blankets from the highway stand
run by a grandfatherly type our aunt
met at her Wednesday night poker game.
But I get no golden bough, and no frilly dress.
Sky-baked rattlers and a beehive out back—
these are my priests, these my mendicant slaves.

It could be worse—a cave is something.
Tangible, dark, damp with sweat and voices.
Sequestered, yes, from the other Oracles,
who weep and beat their curdled breasts
and moan that they are not yet dead,
sequestered from the pretty
young ones with pert noses,
But at least,
in the end,
I was given a cave—
even if the white girls get golden tripods
and dental plans—
it never pays to tell the cavalry
the blankets smell funny.

The *Wheel* goes around, and stops
on the sparkling red-and-white square.
There are animal sounds of delight—
my brother grunts at the prize-refrigerator,
glowing with cleanliness and light.

I just keep chewing my laurel like tobacco,
and the taste is hardly sour at all.

THE ORACLE AT LAS VEGAS

This is how an Oracle sees:

a card, a pair of dice, a spinning coin,
a stone, a rune, a bird's flight,
an organ, a word—

divinity of random selection.
Value is assigned to a group of objects;
one (or more) are chosen at random.
That the luck of the draw
has meaning, holds it like an apple-seed
buried in so much meaningless meat—
this is the source of all divination.

That I draw the Magician
and not the Chariot is significant,
even profound.

That the liver is rotted in a particular pattern,
or *mannaz* is drawn from the rune-bag
instead of *eihwaz*.

That three cherries clatter up from
silver-piped depths, and not lemons,
or sevens, or black bars like gravestones.
This must mean good fortune,
good harvest, many sons,
victory in war. If one random combination
of objects is sacred,
all must be.

                The man from Kansas City
                did not draw the nine of spades
at the emerald blackjack table,
(its velvet-vested keeper stands at attention
in spangled eyeshadow and a bad bleach job—
he does not begin to glimpse the crevice
between her sleek shoes, panting yellow smoke
which rubs her nylon-sheathed calves
with obscene and musk-mouthed insistence)
                instead, his hand is full
                of hearts, bleeding like busts of Mary,
                and the dealer bites her lip,
                whispers amid Babel-towers of
                green and white chips,
                that his wife will leave him for
                an investment banker within the year.

Drowned in the pink neon pools of jackpot
and *sorry, please try again,*

the Oracle is the mouth of probability
and improbability,
opening and closing in the salt tide,
the source of non-random chance—it slides out of her
into the slough of holy objects:
a card, a pair of dice, a spinning coin,
the reeling hexagram-lines of slot machines,
the minor arcana of the blue Bicycle deck.

And behind the glittering palace,
after hours, she climbs into the tin dumpster
to cut open what is left
of the night's prime rib special
searching the ley-lines of gristle and fat
for purpose, for Kansas City and a body
with turquoise lips floating up the Missouri
with a dog-eared nine of hearts
in the back pocket of his jeans.

THE ORACLE AT SEATTLE

Salt-woman, salt-mother
all white, granular
pure and bridal,
diamond capillaries snake through my
cedar branch-body,
a second moon scowls over the lake.
Filled with ether, sulfur, saliva
gasoline and old coffee grounds,
pure ethanol clouds through my skin—
I blush black.

They come in wool-coated evenings
when the sky lies over me
flushed gold and blue—

I am a blister of light.

Locals scrape from my breasts
to pack salmon in the market—
for luck, you understand.
little silver knives graze my collarbone
my sternum
they take and take

happy armfuls of flesh
industrious hands scour me raw.

Dark-faced seals witness
my voice
a shatter of foghorns
sounds from my belly—
a great swollen fish
stuffed with pine nuts and old Coke bottles.

Salt-crone,
I dissolve on slick tongues
gleam on fat fingers
beggars wring words like sweat
from my flesh
and fill up their Styrofoam cups.

I am their own thing
my crystal-skin is owned
clutched
devoured my
mineshaft-mouth—
I am only just enough to feed them all.

THE ORACLE AT ANCHORAGE

Far and far from dark-mooned Tiamat and the Bo Tree
her serpent-mouth flute-like calls
cobalt-crested shadow on rice fields
sibyl of the ice caves close-lipped and solemn.

A little body—palms upturned
to cup tenderly her watery corona
like the smooth head of a child—
his unknowing veins hold her blue beyond the sea
phosphorescence expanding into arteries, ventricles
brimming with ultramarine paraffin. Her hair
flows among the reeds and grasses
the olive and shadowed amber of still water
under the violet-vapored mountain
like a hundred-fingered path.

Where in these glacial curls
will he find the strands of his own capillaries?
His limbs founder in her mane of lapis snow.
This bodied postulant,
a nude and quaking Polaris in the sibyl's eye
due north and terribly separate
arctic, crystal, face a glacial camellia.

He and the slivers of lunar rice are identical in curve and point
but his hand trails unmoving
like silt on the water
as though it were beautiful.

He contemplates her diamond feet
as though he were transparent
on the muddy edge of the stream that ripples
towards the ocean
towards women of plum-blossom robes.
With how many silver-knobbled hands and ruby faces,
cinnamon eyes and soft, ululating voices,
consecrating tongues will they seduce unspeaking
the connecting streams?

He is silent as though he were profound.

But this little body, quiescent meadow
under the mountain
far and far from the copper-bellied bodhisattvas
and the almond eyes of a dozen androgynous devas,
quivers, in the ash-leaf arms of this
little cyanic rice-mother
scoured and washed in blue
the kelp-lipped, oracular mouth enclosing
nut-brown feet and feathered arms
lotus legs, selfless toes.
His body, fluid stone nibbled

by the jade of light and water warm,
planetary breath multiplying throat-tones
into columns of silver.

He and the slivers of stellar rice
are identical in curve and point
but he is animated now by her shadow on the snow
by the flash of a trout under the hooded moon—
awake, invisible
glinting mercurial between hushed trees
extends gentle fingers to stroke her fluted azures and indigos
and open his mendicant mouth.

THE ORACLE AT CHINATOWN

Hexagram 51:
Thunder: coming, frightening, frightening.
After laughing words comes shrieking.

Above the Dim Sum Palace, she sits,
playing pinochle with her grandchildren,
white jade on every gnarl-knuckled finger.
She lets them play for her yarrow stalks
as though they were matchsticks—the eldest
girl is ahead by eleven.

She came from Jiangxi province
with her coins and grass-stalks slung over her back
like a quiver of arrows. She knew nothing
of sibyl-arcana, no swift-footed god
ever glanced over her slim form.
She is a scientist—the yarrow-cast
and coin-throw were precise
as graphs in her hands, broken and whole,
broken and whole: the hexagraphic
morse code.

Her husband joined her the next year,
and they proceeded in the usual way:
three daughters and two sons,
and a small café slung with golden dragons
and a beckoning cat
whose paw sawed the air,
back and forth.

Hexagram 29:
Flowing water arrives at the top. Repeated pit.
Teaches affairs through repetition.

In the store room, between bags
of dumpling-flour and freeze-dried noodles,
heads of cabbage and frozen chickens
hanging from the ceiling like
three-toed pendulums, she squats on the floor
and rolls the stalks against her thigh—
it is a long process, an invisible alchemy
straw into thunder, into water,
into mountains. She counts,
she calculates the ratio of shattered lines
to solid. The numbers flit through her
like black butterflies,
splitting her mouth with wet
and wrinkled wings, antennae
trailing across her molars.

She was surprised to learn that San Francisco
read palms down on Fisherman's Wharf,
a frosted blonde on a wicker tripod
ringed in the raucous barks of sea-lions,
dragging sacred smoke from brown cigars,
and that she called the sun her lover.
                    She never saw the sun most days—
the moon alone witnessed the last over-sugared oolong,
the last fortune of the shift. Occasionally,
she thought she might like
to see the other woman,
ask her why she needed
to tell stories about her flaming bed,
why she wrapped herself up
in those costumes and theatrics,
when a handful of straw suffices.
                    But in the end,
the soup needed spicing.

Hexagram 17:
Thunder in the centre of a marsh: following.
One turns within for solace.

In her kitchen, left in peace by
the throngs who crowd the Wharf-woman,
pressing drachma into her hands, as though that
would make the whole affair authentic—
she is enclosed in steam and sliced fruit;

she is ringed by sheets of gold.
They lay open like a flayed sun,
waiting for her to finish,
the crackle of the yarrow against her skin
echoing wetly in the air.

She holds her pencil with a crooked hand,
recording the numbers,
the thunder and the repeating pit,
the marsh and the horse's womb.
She folds them into the raw dough,
and closes the mouth of the oven
over their light.

THE ORACLE AT MONTEREY

I wore 1985
Bordeaux lipstick
down to the palm-bordered cafe
my limbs gliding through thin rains
towards those civilized polished tables
>   If I did not paint myself with that slick
>   coppery line someone might guess
>   the shape of my mouth—
the inhuman, consumptive
scarlet-stained thread—
these Erinyes-lips.

Behind the steam of frothing milk
this boy with his Narcissus-hair tied back
thinks I am sweet and warm
and that my smile might
taste of cinnamon-chocolate.
Eyes like orange groves in the Pacific sun,
he flashes gentle January teeth—
young and beautiful
dark
intimate in coffee and cream.

But still I redden my mouth
to hide it even from this swan-eyed boy, even from him—

>   that I go mad quietly
>   every morning
>   behind the brass hat racks.

I am the maenadic uvula
expansive in feverlight
watery dimension of pockmarked
coral flesh and tooth quivering
to devour this boy
like Jonah in his feeble reed canoe,
to envelop him in burgundy softness,
to madden him as I am maddened
in a silk-throated ululation.
Ribcage arching like dove-adored
cathedral rafters, these lips
could sacrifice his parchment-limbs
to atavistic whale-gods—
compel fathoms of sea
to cover him in starry waves like a lover,

>   could thrill in the vibrations of his
>   long steely hair against the walls
>   of a moonflower stomach.

I am able to hide it—
the tidal mouth
this organ that seethes in corrosive whispers.

But I carry the boiling brand on my face
smeared with crimson oil—
                bear it like a sacrament
                crusted with garnets and winter rubies
                secretive in runic silences it hums—
slashes of color conceal
with violent necessity:
the incongruity of my presence
in this ordered room of ginger tea and lemon.

The bells of silver coins falling into his
hands with its arcane lines sound in high octaves.
I pull my honey-toned coat around my neck hurrying out into
the wind.
Perhaps he did not see it—
the color opening like a wound   to swallow him
                the polished tables
                the enlightened wallpaper
                 the lemonteacoffeechocolate

swallow them all like the sea.

THE ORACLE AT LOS ANGELES

Play me that old αποθανειν θελω rag,
Σιβυλλα, Σιβυλλα
play me that cage-song with the classic cave motif,
polystyrene granite and the last set-strike of the night,
lemon and gin for the throat, espresso-and-amphetamine
on the faux-gold tripod.

The cymbal-crash and the tin sheet-shake—
it brings the crowds. And the steel wool wig,
the crone costume—who would believe a twenty-something
sibyl?
UCLA postgrad, macrobiotic, orange braids
and *Cosmic Grape* lipstick? It would never sell.
The wrinkled tits and digital voice compression
give the routine that authentic atmosphere,
that Cumaean style.

Sing me τι θελεις, τι θελεις, τι θελεις
last call under the golden bough.
The dry ice smokes impressively—
but the sulfur is real. It clogs the nose like ragweed,
stabs drunkenly at the eyes, dissolves the glue of my falsely
yellowed nails. But the beggar-crowd would never

trust the thin green trail
of the earth's breath into my lungs,
they could not swallow a seer without
the choir bombastic, the plastic Apollo
with Christmas-light eyes and a 40-watt corona
peering out of the shadows.

I play the old pythia-jazz in a Styrofoam temple,
but the ground cracks open just the same—
and after the 7 o'clock show, the 9, and the 11,
it's the same blond god who breaks the dark
and asks his due.

THE ORACLE AT CAYUCOS (CA)

My hair is clean and straight
grey as hyphen of ocean
outside the window,
the tiled floor scrubbed in foamy
blue kitchenlight
sausages frying conversationally with thyme
in a cast iron skillet,
the silver-handled aesthetic of chamomile
and oolong,
steam rising towards the stucco ceiling
like a strangely-versed prayer
whispered over the little copper sun
of my burnished kettle.

I sit as expected,
cross-legged within
the quiet hiss of
leaves like turning pages,
pooled breath of milk and honey
in my little domestic cauldron.

Today I did not scald my palm
on the pan or scorch the meat—
it is something.

There are zucchini and tomatoes
in the garden,
carrots, snap peas, cilantro,
chipotle and poblano peppers
basil and wild mint,
even a new litter of kittens
(black, black, always black
as a cave mouth)—
$10 each.
Take what you can carry. I have nothing
else.

It is gone—
the sulfur with its nicotine hands
has made me asthmatic,
the arcane cave-heat covered
my white arms with psoriasis,
and the laurel leaves
gnashed between my steel-wool teeth
for five decades
have left only anemia
and chipped enamel.

I am closed up like a house.
There is nothing here for you,
nothing in this place
but my clean linoleum and gestating cats,
ascetic kitchen full of vegetables, and
a pair of copper earrings
lying on the vellum pages of a book
I cannot read.

THE ORACLE AT SAN DIEGO

Two girls sit next to me
slightly younger than I
which is to say
they don't remember when
Russia was a swear word
when the mushrooms
we sliced for spaghetti sauce
quivered grimly in the mind.

The girls sit,
sandaled feet propped up
against a scuffed cafe table,
talking as I have talked,
as their friends have talked,
as we all have talked here:

What do you want to be when you grow up?

To what purpose will we bend
the encyclopedic knowledge
of the social order of ants
we acquire through the great
ivy covered breast that wedges

itself into our mouths
with such authority?

And one of them,
the one with turquoise toenails
tosses a sunny curl
over her freckled shoulder like a wind-chime
and says:

Well, you know, I like sort of want
to give something back to the world
but I really don't want to sacrifice anything for myself.

Their skin is California sun-bright
twin golden Buddha-children
plump and happy
with laughing throats and round copper cheeks.
They are Shining
and Beautiful.

Plus, you know, I don't look very good on camera,
so, it makes it hard to be an activist.

Her pretty Gautama-twin beams,
laughing from her belly,
and her plastic earrings dance:

I totally *know what you mean.*

She thoughtfully forks another bite of spinach
into her oystershell mouth
and the word blazes in my brain
like a cathedral.

SACRIFICE

They have filled their laughing bellies
with soybean patties
and dark-leafed organic salad
grown on some mythic sustainable agriculture commune
by utopian, contented Peruvians
with strong teeth and wise eyes.

They have traded in chocolate
and thick yellow cheese
for this dream-produce
putting up an admirable front
of earth conscious activism
so as not to disappoint their parents.

SACRIFICE
SACRIFICE

They live in a dimension I cannot fathom
where saving the earth pays $200,000 a year
and comes with a penthouse apartment
where their orthodontically perfect smiles

can re-grow redwoods
create blue and silver whales from seawater
one touch of their slender fingers
produces synthetic
corn-based gasoline
and their laughter destroys communism
as the laughter of all
American girls should.

It is a breathtaking landscape.

I mean, God, who wants to go dig a ditch in Africa?

Under what cabbage leaf did these women grow,
tan and gleaming?

I think I want to hurt them.

Their innocence is not
starlight-virgin-sweetness
it is just
Emptiness.
A kind of nirvana achieved
not by crossing your legs like river grasses
sitting zazen on a thin reed mat for years
chewing laurel until the tongue bleeds,

but by being born
with a mind smooth and blank
as rice paper
no dark, sinuous ink has traced a thought
across the expanse of it—
it remains
a uniform whiteness
that is almost beautiful,
blazing
like a cathedral.

SACRIFICE
SACRIFICE

I want to give myself to them.
The fat and laughing Buddha
should melt from their cheeks like bronze rain.
I want to bend their sunflower limbs into lotuses
into something other than what they must be.

We are sisters:
We have two faces like a Roman God
One mirthless and solemn,
with large eyes that dance
slowly to the sulfurous dark.
One warm, laughing and beautiful
gold-leaf skin and pearl hands,
but empty

and the scald of the sun
does not follow their steps.

THE ORACLE AT KILAUEA (HI)

Like a Sufi woman
my fingers smell of curry
my hair of saffron
and calloused feet on the embers
of the sky's flaming kiln
I soundless ate two peaches
from some dark-eyed deva's orchard—
feline teeth on that roseate-sulfurous flesh
overlaid by her breath of deathless viridian.

Those beryl hands on my lips, my belly—
damask skin carved by the petroglyphs of ochre mountains
runes of river and snow!

My cedar raft and sails of savage wheat
splintered on the roiling Pacific and there,
past voltaic water,
I found her
glowing calves crossed on a reed mat
lazuli breasts in her hands
cinder-shadows of sinuous leaves
humming on her shoulders.

Her voice the voice of trade winds
albatross on her desolate menhir,
crater-throated her dulcimer mouth
empties into my sternum
wordless—an obelisk of sound—
its edge grooves the bone.

And in candelabra eyes I see myself
in the slick sheen of her dark arms—
my sibling-self
a branch of lurid fruit across her familiar thighs.

And oh, her fennel-stalk fingers hot on my skin!
And oh, her smiling basilisk mouth!

The press of her close,
her breath of cinnamon and plums
she steals my howling womb,
swallows the scarlet grail of my body
like rain
and the wrench of it
convulses through the trees.

She has bound my breasts with the serpent of knowledge
touches my throat
it blooms into brambles and berries—
sexless beneath her perfect hands
I am whole.

We hold the rip and cry of my core between us
like a blood-orange moon
it curves and swells
this giant egg
this temple of self.

Peripheral, the fecund forest
curls and skews.
When again will the river bear me?
Am I now too granite-heavy
To be carried beloved on the star-colored sea?
 But I am rooted by her mouth
fixed by her oceanic torso
belly to belly
singing of otherness
her voice roping around my throat

Between us, we cradle a thing
the gold of its globe erasing
barbaric feet and rice-field hands.
I am affixed like the horn of a moon
and the stars of my teeth are still.

THE ORACLE IN MOTION

1.

The Oracle at Rhode Island
her hair snapping in the snow
like willow branches
removes a measured toe
from the froth and juniper spray of the Atlantic
clattering lobster and gulping mackerel
fall from her yucca bell heels.

Kelp-ringed fingers carefully
fold a red paper napkin
and lay it alongside a little cairn of quahog shells,

knead   a poultice of moss and wild basil
and paint thinner
to seal up her fluted sternum
where she is separating like
the perforated edge
of a past due electric bill,
knowing the taste of what is coming
like laurel leaves in her mouth.

She cuts a winter coat from a Franciscan's cowl
washes it in ashes and lye
and cutting waxen wind with her lashes,
covers her hair.

She unbolts her oleander mouth
and begins to eat the broken
yellow lines of US 95 South,
swallowing the K'un hexagram:

the earth opening like the belly of a mare.

2.

Snow hunts us
bleach-breasted and with thighs
cupped to receive our night-teas
oolong and peppermint in roadside crockery
refusing to say that
this is a descent
out of the New England
we made grinning
with clay-spattered hands—

where our bathtub would not drain
and the ceiling was cracked

where we had a wooden fruit-bowl
and clay sake-cups

where I cleaned the mirrors
and the bed-sheets

where we let stray kittens sleep
on our kitchen table
and I kept violets in a silver vase

where the last leaves clung like red envelopes
hiding barnacle-tongued fortunes
to the knuckled elms.

3.

A hoarse rope is sawing her belly in half
she vomits white cardamom
and oyster shells
into the floorboards of a 1986 Dodge pick-up.

Mangled guard rails
wrap around her waist
like a coin belt.

The road is entering her,
replacing him,
moving its tarred body over her legs

her chrysanthemum back
arches under the weight
of asphalt and broken glass
and the sky like a cut throat.

From her black sleeve she draws
The Magician
and slices her finger on its lunar edge.
It is not her card, but his.

4.

Under stars like shattered teeth
we leave the Ozarks
snow falling like milk from a glass pitcher
on hulking black hipbones and jaws
jutting at our shoulders.

You touch my denim knee when you downshift
and the plains open out like a book of the dead
frozen and sparkling
in our headlights.

We are bringing the winter west—
scowling snow hounds us
bearing black branches
mixed with myrrh in rose quartz
reliquaries

mixed with bits
of my bone and your hair
calcifying in the dark.
(It is over, it is over
and we are traveling to a place
where you can allow yourself
to leave me behind—)

The hawthorn trees have spun
a second skin of ice
and you take a picture of me
knowing it will be one of the last,
laughing under their boughs like silver skates.

5.

She binds her breasts with tea leaves
stuffs darjeeling and orange pekoe down her throat,
dragging winter behind her like a penance.

She becomes a papier-mâché
Yuki-Onna, Lady of Snow and Death
on agate knees
in classical dress
her body becomes a hymn
calling storms out
from the ventricles of the moon

to drown the highway spooling out before her
like black rope.

She flicks a brown stream of earl grey
onto the concrete
charting in nautical miles
the polygonal fortune
of her own path westward—
the aesthetic of the left woman.

Cutting a eucharist from her kidneys
she offers it to her lover's tongue,
double-vision bending her like
an obscene origami.
He takes it warmly because he thinks
it is a coin for the Coke machine.

6.

We skip the Grand Canyon.

A line of hotel swimming pools
ripple out
like coronal sapphires
through the Arizona palm trees
and in the coral-pillowed morning
your skin smells like sweat and chlorine.

We sleep through two alarms.
While you run to the corner cafe
for coffee with two sugars
and banana muffins
I stand with eyes like fists
at the window
(we are already separating like cream)
watching the sun burn its alphabet into the sky.

7.

The woman weeps skullcap and mugwort
staining her lap with
penitential water rings
that seethe into her skin
like boiling oil.

She smashes her rune-stones against the windshield
screaming through the blood
of her hands.

8.

California takes us in
lying under the latitudes
like a fat golden seal.
There is bougainvillea
spilling over lemon leaves

and we eat blood oranges
from your grandmother's tree
quietly on the beach.

Your body folding against mine
fears to say
now that the snow is gone—
it is the end.
Gold dust seeps from our
separate palms.
The blown veils of cloud attend as
I begin to tell your fortune
on the sand of crushed topaz—
the wind shuffles the cards
with tattooed hands.

The road surrounds us
like a dark nova
but it is over
the water
covers my heels
in blue.

EPILOGUE:
THE ORACLE DEPARTS

She rides her witch's chariot home through the humid summer night, starless and black, with her Tarot deck in a pouch at her waist. Is she suddenly now a woman and no longer an Oracle? Is there a metamorphosis of flesh and light when the dark little rooms vanish and the chant is over? Does she still taste laurel and volcanic bile in her mouth, thirsty and burning, as her little shift ends and there is an empty hut looming white and sullen ahead of her? Of course, it is not hers; it is the Oracle's house, tucked away into the southern quadrant of the city where it will not bother anyone, two rooms and a leaking roof, and the lingering smell of all those dead women, their sweat and their breath, their blood and their footsteps, their ghost-cells floating like dust in the stale air.

She remembers that there is a half-filled bottle of wine and a bunch of old grapes in the refrigerator.

And on the way to this seclusion, she is engulfed by those who have stood before her while she crouched over a sulfurous fissure, chanting nonsense and chewing dusty green leaves with aching teeth. They do not greet her in the marketplace, they do not congratulate her on a well-finished work-week. They do not offer her a special price on cheese or milk, or ask her to stop by for a bit of tea next Thursday. But they crowd her wheels, even prodding the spokes with olive-branches, begging her for predictions when she is off-duty, just little ones, madam, just nothing-at-all answers: will the new child will be a boy or a girl, will it rain on the festival days, will the oxen bought last month be strong and docile?

She is not allowed to go and sit in the theatre, watch the latest comedies involving wicked and clever servants with a glass of cold retsina. Visiting dignitaries scowl and change their seats when she settles herself on the stone bench. She might wince with some kind of terrible half-memory when the voice of an actor bellows out, playing the part of her patron—it is not good for ticket sales. It discomfits folk to see her sitting in the stands, hands folded in her lap, dressed in modest rose and black, instead of her child's dress, the symbol of her thrall to the fissure, or the sun—it is hard for her to remember which owns her—the sky or the bottomless earth? She supposes that the dress means she is his child, the sun's helpless daughter who must bear him on her back, though he burns her so. But the earth's exhalations enter her like a husband, invade her womb with steam-children whose dead eyes flash sulfurous and toxic. She cannot decide which should be called her jailor—but it doesn't matter, much.

She does not want to go to the theatre, anyway. The confusion would well up in her like ink drawn into a pen—she does not remember what she has said during her trances. How can she know for which farmer she has predicted rain and high wheat, and which famine? Not knowing for which empire she has encapsulated ruin, for which woman still-birth? Perhaps those who have heard what they wished to hear would want to give her gifts of gold and wool, of honeyed sweets and paint for her teeth—those sour plants leave such a stain. Others might pinch her as the chorus came singing onto the stage, or slap her as she passed, or worse, cut her throat in a black alley, so that she could not speak desolation again.

In her, the zucchini and olives wither before they are planted, the wine sours before it ferments, the daughters die in childbirth before their conception. What noble lady would have an Oracle at her evening bridge club? What song would she be allowed to sing at the festivals, when all fear the gravelly tones of her voice? At what altar could she leave a beaded gown or bough of swollen black olives as sacrifice? She is herself a sacrifice, slaughtered on the navel-stone for the prosperity of this town that thrives on its prophetess, whose bustling spice trade and oxen market is based upon her body, whose politics sprout from her brow like an empty suit of armor? She is the burnt offering to the terrible light of the sun god. She has a shadow-life, annihilated by Castalia, searing her throat like acid, removing all that is woman from her.

But when she is wrong, when she predicts that the war will be lost, when the proud ships return and discredit her with their raucous victory, she is loathed. The village will grow poorer, will be able to fund fewer festivals. Less and less often will leaders come to consult the Oracle, and the gifts to the temple will be suddenly meager, little more than rotten barley and worm-riddled peaches. She narrowly escaped stoning in the narrow streets, and among the purpled faces were the priests who just yesterday exalted her.

And she will not be mourned when pretty Americans come with their backpacks to wander over the temple and the old theatre, musing over anything at all but her huddled form in her little room with that savage hole in the world, its sallow smoke concealing her face like a nun's veil.

And so, she breathed the unforgiving air and the sacred water for the last time, then turned her back on the temple. She collected her half-bottle of wine and her withered grapes into a satchel, folded her baby-dress with its pink ribbons and obscene frill around the glass and fruit, and walked west out of the city, walked west to the sea, west across the mountains and light-drenched plains.

The sun settled onto her head like a red hand.

AUTHOR'S NOTE

For the span of a summer and an autumn, just after I had graduated from college and could, for the first time in years, stop thinking in Greek, I was employed as a Tarot reader in the sleepy seaside town of Newport, Rhode Island. It was an almost laughably mythic situation: I was closed up in a hot, murky room at the top of a very tall stone tower whose windows were covered in ivy. The room was a storage space for a local theatre company, and so was crammed to the gills with strange props, while the walls were covered in spare curtains, red and black velvet complete with gold pulls.

That year, I spent my days as an Oracle.

And as I played this role, I could not help but feel that I was connected to those other women, those strange and beautiful creatures whose names were subsumed in the much larger names of their cities: *Delphi. Dodona. Cumae.* Maybe I was even one of them. I began to think: what does an Oracle do in her off-hours? What does an Oracle do when she retires? How does an Oracle become an Oracle? Of course, to some extent, ancient texts have answers to these questions. Historians and priests wrote down the job requirements and the average life cycle. But no one ever asked an Oracle.

Of course, the site of Delphi is empty now, and visitors are no longer even allowed to approach the temple. But for me, that place is full of ghosts. Full of Pythias who spent lifetimes performing a complex ventriloquism, speaking not for themselves, but for their god. The year of my oracular tower I returned to America from Europe, and to California from New England. In a very few steps, I accomplished the mileage of classical progress—Old World to New, East to West. And I would like to think that I brought a wraith or two with me. This book, in truth, is a small libation to them, a tragic cycle, finally, for that nameless Chorus of Sibyls.

Printed in the United States
31236LVS00001B/184-192